# Fiona's Luck

Teresa Bateman

*Illustrated by*

Kelly Murphy

Charlesbridge

*For Stephanie, Shannon, and Emma—*
*When challenged, they lift up their chins.*
*They know luck is grand,*
*And can give you a hand,*
*But they also know*
*Cleverness wins.*
*—T. B.*

*To my grandparents, the Brodericks and Howleys, the McAdams and Murphys*
*—K. M.*

2009 First paperback edition
Text copyright © 2007 by Teresa Bateman
Illustrations copyright © 2007 by Kelly Murphy
All rights reserved, including the right of reproduction in whole or in part in any form.
Charlesbridge and colophon are registered trademarks of Charlesbridge Publishing, Inc.

Published by Charlesbridge
85 Main Street
Watertown, MA 02472
(617) 926-0329
www.charlesbridge.com

**Library of Congress Cataloging-in-Publication Data**
Bateman, Teresa.
Fiona's luck / Teresa Bateman ; illustrated by Kelly Murphy.
p. cm.
Summary: A clever woman named Fiona must pass the leprechaun king's tests
when she tries to get back all the luck he has locked away from humans.
ISBN: 978-1-57091-651-9 (reinforced for library use)
ISBN: 978-1-57091-643-4 (softcover)
[1. Leprechauns—Fiction. 2. Luck—Fiction. 3. Ireland—Fiction.]
I. Murphy, Kelly, 1977- ill. II. Title.
PZ7.B294435      Fio 2007
[E]—dc22
2006009027

Printed in China
(hc) 10 9 8 7 6 5 4 3 2
(sc) 10 9 8 7 6 5 4 3 2 1

Illustrations done in acrylic, watercolor, and gel medium on coventry rag
Display type and text type set in Ossian and Galliard
Color separations by Chroma Graphics, Singapore
Printed and bound by Jade Productions
Production supervision by Brian G. Walker
Designed by Diane M. Earley

Once, luck was as free to be had in Ireland as sunlight, and just as plentiful. It filled the air, and anyone could grab a handful of it as the need arose. This was largely due to the leprechauns, for they made luck like cows made milk.

Then the big folk arrived in Ireland. They were
so large, the luck clung to them wherever they went.
"Something will have to be done," the king of
the leprechauns declared. "We can't have those huge
people soaking up all of the luck. What would be
left for us?"

So, under the king's orders, the leprechauns wove
fine golden thread into magical nets. Then, late one
midsummer's eve, when the luck was at its height,
they swept it up and stored it all in an oak chest by
the king's throne, so he could distribute it where
and when he chose.

But the leprechauns had been too thorough.
They not only scooped up all the leprechaun luck, but
any other luck that had been floating about as well.
    The land of Ireland fell into a time of great
misfortune. Hens gave no eggs, and cows would
not let down their milk. The potatoes rotted in
the ground.

Now it happened that in Ireland there lived a woman named Fiona. She knew the lack of luck had to be the work of the leprechauns. So it followed that they alone could restore good fortune to the land.

But getting luck back from a leprechaun would be like squeezing water from a stone—not that it can't be done, but it usually requires more strength than you're apt to have. Sometimes cleverness, though, is worth more than strength.

So Fiona took her last coins and used them to buy a cow and some chickens. Then, every morning and evening, she would take that cow into the barn. When she emerged, she would be carrying two buckets slopping over with whiteness.

"Aye, she's a fine cow," Fiona would say to any who asked. "It's lucky I am to have her."

Soon the rumors began—while others were short on luck, Fiona had pails of it.

Every morning Fiona would go into the chicken
coop and emerge with her covered basket bulging
with curves.

"The hens seem contented," she commented to
her neighbors. "It's lucky I am to have them."

Soon the rumors spread—while others were
short on luck, Fiona had baskets of it.

Then Fiona began digging in her garden and filling her wheelbarrow with round, dirt-covered lumps.

"It's not a good year for potatoes," Fiona said to all who passed. "Still, I'm lucky to have what I have."

Now the rumors had wings—while others were short on luck, Fiona had wheelbarrows full of it.

Naturally, word of this unexpected luck made its
way to the leprechaun king.

One day Fiona was walking across a green meadow
when she suddenly found herself surrounded by a
small crowd of the fair folk. In a trice they grasped
the hem of her skirt and ran around her in a circle.
She turned, to keep the skirt from wrapping around
her knees, and as she turned, the landscape blurred.
When it sharpened again, Fiona found herself
beneath the earth, in the throne room of the
leprechaun king.

It was a glorious cavern, with rich tapestries hanging against tall granite walls, and the floor cobbled entirely of jewels. Torches and candlelight made everything sparkle, and music filled the air.

In front of Fiona stood the throne, and on the throne sat the leprechaun king.

He beckoned to her.

Fiona approached, her eyes scanning the room for the missing luck. She was as sure as smoke loves fire that the king would be keeping it close to himself. As she curtsied, she spied the oak chest. It was glowing slightly—sealed by a spell, since everyone knows that no lock can hold luck for long.

"What would you be wanting of me?" Fiona asked politely.

The king scowled. "Where are you getting all your luck? Who's been giving it to you, and why?" he demanded.

Fiona's eyes widened in innocence. "I have no luck," she declared. "Indeed, here I am, a captive of the leprechauns. If that's luck, you can take it."

"So, you claim to have no luck?" the king inquired, raising an eyebrow. "Well, let's put it to the test. And when I prove that you've lied to me, as forfeit I'll take all the luck you have and put it with the rest that I guard." His eyes flicked toward the chest.

Fiona frowned. "That's a sorry bargain for me," she said, "yet I know the rules. If a test is to be made, then a forfeit must be paid by the loser. I haven't lied, so when I'm proved truthful, I demand a wish as your forfeit."

The king's eyes turned shrewd. "Agreed," he said slyly. "I'll give you a wish for exactly the value of the luck you have, if my tests prove me wrong."

Fiona knew she was being cheated. A woman with wit, though, can turn even a leprechaun's cleverness against himself. She glanced at the chest and then, barely keeping a smile from her lips, nodded.

So the agreement was made. At the king's gesture, one of his magicians brought out a low table and placed upon it three beautiful shells. Under one he hid a small gold coin. Then he whisked the shells around and over and under in a blur no human eye could follow.

"Now," the king said. "Where's the gold?"

There was one chance in three of her picking correctly, and a person with good luck would find the gold every time. Even a person with a little luck would find the gold occasionally. But though they played the game over and over again, Fiona could never locate the coin. It was as if she had no luck at all.

"Another test," the king ordered.

A leprechaun harp was brought forth. Now, leprechaun instruments make music by the luck of the player. A person with good luck would be able to play something just by stroking the strings. Even a person with just a hint of luck could probably finger out a simple melody. But in Fiona's hands the strings went out of tune, and no matter how she stroked and plucked, nothing but ear-bending noise resulted.

The king shuddered and frowned. Could he have been mistaken? Perhaps the last test would prove him right.

"Bring out the chess set!" he demanded.

He and Fiona faced each other across the board. The king made his opening move. Nobody could hope to beat the leprechaun king, for he was steeped in luck. But a person with good luck could last a while against him. Even a person with just a bit of luck had hopes of making a few good moves.

Despite the king trying his hardest to lose, Fiona was beaten soundly within two minutes.

The king eyed her in amazement. "You have no luck at all!" he declared. "But what about the milk, and the eggs, and the potatoes?"

Fiona sighed. "If I fill my milk bucket with whitewash, or my egg basket with pinecones, or my wheelbarrow with dirty rocks, surely that's my own business? I told you I had no luck, and I didn't lie. Now I'll take my wish and be on my way."

The king nodded slowly. "Indeed, I did promise you a wish, but for exactly the value of the luck you actually had. You've proven to me that you have no luck at all, so that's all you can wish for—nothing!"

He smiled at the cleverness of his reasoning, all well within the limits of leprechaun law. Then his smile wavered—for Fiona was smiling too.

"So I can wish for nothing?" she asked.

He nodded, puzzled.

"Then I wish for a hole," Fiona continued. "A hole is nothing, after all, and that's exactly the value of my wish. I wish for a hole that will never go away, and I wish it to be in the lid of that chest!"

She pointed to the chest of luck by the king's throne.

The power of a wish, rightfully earned, is not to be denied. A hole appeared in the chest, and luck began escaping immediately.

The king howled with rage, but what could he do? He had made a bargain and was forced to keep it. With an angry wave of his hand, Fiona was whirled away. When she opened her eyes, she was back in the meadow, the sun just rising over the hills. If there was an extra sparkle to the sunshine, and the grass glowed greener than before, well, it was only to be expected.

And that is why, from that day to this, you'll always find some luck roaming free around Ireland. For the hole is still in the chest and the king must keep his promise.

But as for Fiona—well, as she herself said, "Luck's all well and good, but myself? I'd rather depend on my wits."